Me and My Brother

Annick Press Ltd.

We acknowledge the support of the Canada Council for the Arts, the Ontario Arts Council, and the Government of Canada through the Book Publishing Industry Development Program (BPIDP) for our publishing activities.

Cataloging in Publication

Ohi, Ruth
        Me and my brother / Ruth Ohi.

"A Ruth Ohi picture book".
ISBN 978-1-55451-092-4 (bound)
ISBN 978-1-55451-091-7 (pbk.)

        I. Title.

PS8579.H47M35 2007   jC813'.54   C2007-901398-8

The art in this book was rendered in watercolor.
The text was typeset in Animated Gothic Light.

Distributed in Canada by: Published in the U.S.A. by:
Firefly Books Ltd.   Annick Press (U.S.) Ltd.
66 Leek Crescent   Distributed in the U.S.A. by:
Richmond Hill, ON   Firefly Books (U.S.) Inc.
L4B 1H1   P.O. Box 1338
                                   Ellicott Station
                                   Buffalo, NY 14205

Printed in China.

Visit us at: www.annickpress.com

Me and My Brother

Ruth Ohi

annick press
toronto + new york + vancouver

For best-friend-brothers everywhere
—R.O.

Brother in the kitchen.

Brother in the sun.

Brother sitting still.

Brother on the run.

Time to go home.

Brother with my best toy.

Brother with my cap.

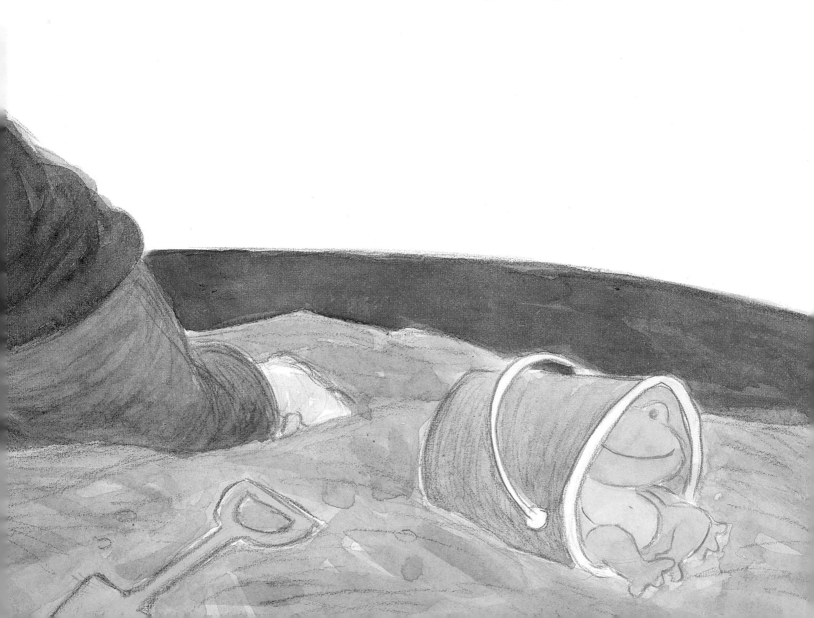

Here's my little brother ...

... waking from his nap.